SILENCE

Elijah Ling

Contents

Prologue

Z eal let out a deep, frustrated sigh. Her honey brown eyes darted here and there as she listened to the cop on the other end of the phone line. His tedious rant of her being carefree went in one ear and out the other. There was someone out there, watching her every move, and she was damn sure of it.

She could barely catch the last sentence that the cop had said before silence reigned; one that was utter and absolute. Zeal ran her thin, bony fingers through her lengthy brown hair, and sighed for the umpteenth time. The man was proving difficult, telling her she was just imagining things when she knew very well that she was not. How could she be wrongly accused of something she was well aware of? That was not right.

He hounded Zeal with questions, but she could pay no attention to what he was saying.She flipped the shutters of the window and stared outside. It was cloudy and it looked like a storm was about to come. The sky was gray and gave the street a sad outlook. The wind fluttered the leaves and flowers wildly. Zeal could hear the roof making cringing noises. She clung to the telephone that was on her ear as she saw a silhouette in the darkness, all dressed in black.

He stood afar, unruffled by the wind as his eyes seemed to pierce through her. An eerie chill went up her spine, eliciting an involuntary gasp as she violently snapped the shutters close.

"I am telling you, there really is someone watching me." Zeal's voice trembled, desperation clawing at the edges. She was scared and pertrified at the same time. Fear trickled down the small of her back and made her curl her toes.

The cop heaved a sigh in frustration.

"We have gone over this a couple of times," he said. She could hear the slight agitation in his voice.

"Fine, if that's what you say, then it's okay," she said, her voice crisp and sharp. "But if anything does happen to me or my kid, you would be very well held responsible." That said, she hung up the call.

She blew out a breath and her eyes watered and tears fell in loops from the corners. She felt frustrated due to the fact that the cops weren't even giving her case the much needed attention that it deserved.

Zeal decided to peep out of the window again. There the figure was, across the street still standing and watching her. Goosebumps appeared on her skin and she shivered. She rubbed her bare arms to reduce the chill that had spread from her head to her toes. It was not from the cold, but from the deadly eyes of someone who she thought was a killer.

Someone was definitely out there, watching her and waiting for an opportunity to kill her. She didn't know what or why the person was after her. But she wasn't going to cower or shy away from what was to come. She would face it for one reason; to ensure the safety of her kid.

A thin coat of light blanketed the sky followed by an ear-piercing scream that caused her to subconsciously shiver. This was because, the thunder so happened to flood the clouds just as someone stepped in front of her view. Zeal wrapped her cream, colored sweater tighter around her body and staggered away from the window. She headed for her daughter's room.

Chapter 1

Zeal's POV

I drummed my fingers lightly on the steering wheel, awaiting the closing time for my daughter's school. I craned my neck after a while, and checked the time. It was already two o'clock. I had been waiting for quite a while, and was growing a bit weary.

I looked across the street at kids playing with their balloons and mothers that guided them with caution. I could also see a guy at the street corner, stringing a guitar and singing a sad song. For a minute, I forgot my aim and got lost in the scenery before me. I only got out of my trance when I heard the clang of the school's gate.

I spotted the security man opening it and I removed my car keys from the ignition, and got out. It was finally time. I saw the flock of kids that ran out from the school, some running to the school's playground and others merely stood. Some stared afar off with their school bags; probably waiting for their parents to pick them up.

A wave of relief engulfed me when I spotted my little angel with a girl that she held on tightly to. Her other hand was linked with a brown-haired lady who was her class teacher.

I placed my right hand on my jaw and stared at my child in wonder. When had she grown so fast? She was indeed my world. I had laboured so much in giving birth to her, and exactly two years later, my husband took his last breath. His death was a complete mystery to me, and ever since then, I vowed never to let my precious baby slip from my fingers, just like my husband did.

I saw Lisie squinting her eyes, with a hand on her forehead, searching with diligence for me. It was indeed a hot, sunny afternoon and I was perspiring through my armpit in my brown–long sleeved shirt. She spotted me and shouted in glee, running over to me. I felt like a proud mom and carried my five-year-old daughter in my arms. I patted her blonde hair and kissed her forehead.

She giggled and pecked me on the cheek. Her blue eyes caught the golden rays of the sun, and I marvelled at how beautiful she looked. I saw her class teacher approach us and I gave a broad smile. The young woman was called Glee. She was popular; in all likelihood that she was always cheerful and loved to play with the kids but, her looks didn't really fit her name.

Her nose was a bit crooked, her hair a shade too brown. Big google glasses that probably weren't medicated, sat atop her nose. Her eyes were impossible not to notice. They were a light, honey coloured brown.

She nodded her head in appraisal at me, and I cleared my throat to speak.

"Good afternoon, Glee," I greeted in good cheer. "Hope Lisie didn't give you any trouble?"

I ruffled her hair and let her out of my grasp. I noticed that as soon as she left my arms, she clutched the hands of a girl that looked to be a bit older than her. She had green eyes, and a pretty face. I made a mental note to ask about that, and turned to pay full attention to Glee.

The class teacher droned on and on about how Lisie, my daughter, was quite an armful. How she answered all the questions that were asked in class, and also about how she was full of fun and high spirit.

Okay, well, I couldn't blame her. It was a new start for her after all.

"But I really do like her excitement towards learning," the teacher concluded.

"Well that's good," I said nodding my head in appreciation. "At least she is adapting to her new environment."

The teacher lowered and raised her head in agreement. Lisa kept jumping up and down, dragging my hand whilst begging for my attention.

"Mummy," she cooed. "Meet my new friend." She was looking at me earnestly, wanting to know my opinion of her companion. I blew a strand of hair away from my face, my eyes brimming with anxiety.

I crouched down to their height and studied the kid for a short while. She seemed shy. Her head was bent, and she used her feet to graze the ground slightly, but there was something odd about her. Her matted hair was streaked with dirt as if she just arrived from a jungle.

I could feel the teacher's eyes on me.

"What's your name?" I asked using my hand to lift her chin, so I could stare into her puppy green eyes.

"Bennie," was all she said. I rubbed my palms on my black jeans and stood up. I turned to the teacher to ask some questions; questions that were flooding my mind and needed answers.

"Who is this?" I asked her, furrowing my brows.

"About that," she started. "I don't really know... Lisa has been clinging to Bennie since classes started."

What? And I was only just noticing that. I mentally face palmed myself and called out to Lisa who had run to go play with her new found friend, Bennie some distance away.

She came running and jumped excitedly into my arms. I held her briefly and told her we needed to get going. She furrowed her brows and frowned her pretty face. Gosh, she looked so adorable.

"I don't want to go," she said in a pleading voice. "I want to stay and play with Bennie."

I looked towards Bennie who was building a castle with sand, and sighed. Now, this was going to be a whole lot complicated. I looked to the class teacher with pleading eyes. She called out to Bennie and held her hand in hers. I ordered Lisa to close her eyes and told her, I had a surprise for her. She squealed in excitement and closed them.

I whispered for the teacher to take Bennie away and she did that. I could hear the noise of kids playing in the playground to the left of me as I turned and headed for my car; my hands still around Lisa's eyes.

"Can I open 'em now," she pleaded. By the time, I was already at my car.

"Sure you can," I replied. She opened her eyes and looked round; eager to find the surprise I had for her. When she saw nothing, she screamed aloud, and kicked her chubby little legs. My face broke into a smile and I forced her into the back seat of the car as she kept on screaming for Bennie. What was up with my kid and this Bennie girl?

I closed the door and hurried to enter the driver's seat before Lisa would create a mess. I had just got in when she began throwing her school bag all over the place; her books flying in every direction. I was getting scared of the tantrum Lisa was creating.

I slid into the driver's seat and shut the door, ordering Lisa to stay put as I twisted up and bent over my seat, to buckle her seat belt.

I continued to observe Lisa through the rear-view mirror that was between my seat, and the passenger's seat. She would throw her tantrums occasionally and I would get a bit scared, because of course, this was all new to me and I wasn't used to it.

"Did you eat the lunch I packed for you, Lisie?" I asked.

I could see her scrunching up her face and she folded her arms across her small frame. I turned to stare at her in brief.

"Hey! Watch it!" someone yelled, and I speedily tried to regain control of the car.

"Sorry!" I yelled back sticking my head a bit out of the window.

I was back to keeping my attention on the road and I gripped the steering wheel, my knuckles turning white.

"I asked you a question, young lady!" I demanded.

"I didn't eat it," she said in her tiny voice.

I blew out my breath. I had taken great care in preparing lunch for my baby and she deemed it fit not to eat it. What were the odds of that?

I stared at her briefly through the car mirror again, and asked her why she had refused to eat her food.

"My class teacher didn't feed me." I heard her purr.

I sighed in disbelief.

"Your class teacher what...?" I asked furrowing my brows, my voice a bit uneven. "Haven't I told you to learn how to eat by yourself?"

"Uhhnnn," she answered. "But I really wanted someone to feed me." I saw her bobbing her head.

I shook my head, just as I pulled the car to a stop, in front of the red traffic light. Turning to stare at Lisie, I made sure that her seatbelt was cinched properly. I didn't want to hear any stories and I wasn't counting on losing anyone so dear to me, anytime soon.

The car beside me suddenly honked aloud and I turned to stare. A formidable man with a muscular build sat behind the wheel. His jawline was sharp and jarring, with a thin line of beard that ran the side of his face. I couldn't help but sigh. It had been a long time since I had a man, all to myself. Ever since my husband's death.

"Mummy." I could hear my kid say. "Am I getting too old?"

I laughed at that and surged the car forward just as the light turned green. My baby was just the perfect age for me. At five years, she was a bundle of joy and excitement.

The car that had been beside me took the left turn, while I took the right. Too bad, in all likelihood, I would not see him again. I noticed the car was a bit quiet, and I checked on my kid through the mirror. She had fallen asleep and her blonde hair stuck to her face. I could see beads of sweat on her forehead and I stretched my right hand to turn on the air conditioner; keeping the left on the wheel. Cold air blasted through and enveloped the car.

I was enjoying the feel of it as I relaxed in my seat and turned on the radio. My favourite jam was playing and I nodded my head in sync with the music.

I drove all the way home and made a stop only to fill my car, at the gas station.

Chapter 2

Zeal's POV

I could hear the natural chirping of birds as sunlight streamed in through the trees. The sky seemed clear and was a crystal blue colour. I looked up and whirled round in circles as a gentle gust of wind, kissed my cheeks. I loved the scenery that was before me. The streams of water flowing could be heard in the distance and I noted something in mute. There was no other noise. Everywhere was absolutely quiet; that is, apart from nature taking control.

I made a mental note of this and began walking forward, my feet crunched the pale fallen leaves. I tried not to make a sound and it was because I didn't want to disturb the cycle of nature. As I made my way to the stream, leaves continued to fall.

When I got there, I sucked up the beauty as I took it all in. Water gushed out from an opening in the huge crevice rock and despite the noise it made, I could still feel that sense of quiet. That stillness and calm. I breathed in the fresh air and sighed. It was all so peaceful and refreshing. This place was where utter silence existed, where only nature was allowed to take control, where humans avoided, and where creatures ate those who disturbed it.

I looked at my shoulder where a leaf had fallen. I held the gold coloured, veiny leaf, in my hand. It looked so natural, just like the fallen spring. In the distance, I could hear a machine sound aloud. What? Who the hell has come to disturb this peace? I thought. I could hear a child screaming in the distance and calling for help.

This was what the creatures did to you if you disturbed the silence. I stared at the sky with the leaf in my hand and saw flocks of bat-like creatures heading to where I could hear the scream. It all seemed so surreal. This wasn't right; I didn't want someone to die because, they didn't know how to keep the silence. They were likely travellers and had stopped by the way to get something to eat.

I flung the single leaf I had been holding and hurried with light footsteps across the thick forest. I didn't want to make any noise so the creatures would not come for me. As I approached where I could hear the continuous screaming, I decided that the only way I could help was to shout and take cover so their attention would be all on me. At least the human that was out there would be safe for the meantime.

I gave a loud scream and all at once, the creatures headed in my direction. That I noticed by the cacophony of sounds of the bat's wings, through the trees. I ran, immediately taking cover in the near-by bush; not waiting till they got to me. And as I crouched behind the thick bush I could feel the bat-like creature's breath so close to me. I stilled, too afraid to move, and I spotted another of the same creature through an open clearing in the leaves. Its ears were wide open, waiting to hear any sound.

I knew there were more out there. I could feel them.

After a while of waiting, I saw the creature fly high in the sky. It's wings sprouting from it's contorted body. I released the breath I didn't know I had been holding and waited for when I would make my next move.

I woke up with a start. My alarm that was by the bedside table gave a shrill cry, and I groaned aloud. I knew this nightmare would leave me disgruntled and make my day one heck of a mess.

Chapter 3

Zeal's POV

It was past five when I finally pulled up at the gas station. Last I had checked, there was someone at the pumps. But now, the whole place just looked a bit deserted and quiet.

That was strange.

Shrugging that thought out of my mind, I clambered out of the car, stepped onto the pavement, and turned to make sure my kid was secured.

She was sleeping soundly and snoring a bit. That in itself was odd. Lisie never snored unless she was very tired. I closed my car door and walked steadily to the pumps. There stood a shop a bit to my left with the 'Closed' signpost and, I made a mental note to check on that, the next time I drove by.

I was in the process of filling my tank, when I noticed a dark clothed figure at the far corner of the store. The hooded outline was staring right at me and I tried my best to hurry, fumbling here and there.

I felt a slight chill run down my spine to the small of my back and I shivered in fear.Before I could finish, I turned back to where I had seen the figure and saw it had vanished right out of sight.

Feeling a bit relieved, I heaved a sigh, and covered the tank, screwing the lid in place. What I didn't foresee when I turned to enter my car, was the figure standing so close, and looking through the windshield.

What was he looking at?

I bit my nails in panic and could only hope that Lisie was safe in the car.

My shirt clung to my body and my hands started to get a bit clammy with sweat. I approached my car slowly but, the figure stood unwavering. When I got to the driver's door, I hurried in and shut it, putting the lock in place.

Now, this time, the dark coated figure appeared directly in front of my car and, it took every bit of willpower to keep my heart rate from plummeting into my stomach. The head was bent, and hands in the confines of his pockets. I turned back to check if Lisie was still sleeping and found her turning to the left, trying to position herself properly. She continued snoring all the while, and I felt a bit calm, reassured that my kid was okay.

I began laying on the horn at the figure and for a while, he kept still in that same posture.

What the hell was going on?

I gritted my teeth trying not scream, as I smashed my fist into the horn repeatedly. At the fourth horn, Lisie jerked, clearly awoken and then, started crying. I was getting scared, my anxiety growing by the minute. The figure's head began to raise slightly; I presumed it was at the sound of a child's voice.

"Shh, shh, shhhh," I cooed, using my right hand to rub her legs, while I kept my eyes on the road. Lisie eventually calmed down and, the figure vanished right out of sight. It was only then, with the threat no longer present, I became aware that I had been holding my breath the entire time and, slowly let out a heavy exhale.

Setting my car into motion, I drove at an alarming rate and decided not to make any more stops, till I got home.

My house was located close to a cliff- reason being that I loved the peace, quiet, and also the serene environment. Although it got creepy at night; at times I could see a black cloaked figure staring at me and that usually gave me chills that ran up my spine.

I was a bit scared and had made frantic calls to the police department a few times to send a surveillance vehicle to patrol the area. However, they were being adamant on the fact that I had not been physically attacked and that through one of their futile searches, they couldn't find anything.

I was growing weary of having to get up at nights for no reason, only to stare at the black clothed figure that always stood right outside my window. I was thinking perhaps- maybe it was time we moved.

But I knew that would affect my baby, Lisie, it was hard already with us moving to a new place due to the death of my husband and it was taking a toll on the poor kid.

I had been really devastated by his demise. He had been someone so dear to my heart, someone that stood by me, someone I cared for and loved and someone who made me give birth to such a wonderful child. I was indeed grateful for that. And to this day, his death was still a mystery and left at that.

I remember that fateful day I had been notified of his accident. He had been heading on a journey the day before. But he never came back.

I had rushed to the hospital where he was admitted and stayed by him till he took his last breath. He had been suffering for a week, trying to battle with the claws of death; needless to say, it had been cruel. I was going through pains just watching my husband groaning day after day, and writhing with body pangs.

He was given painkillers but it did nothing to surpress the intense pain I knew he felt inside. I cried night after night, praying to God that his sickness would go away. The doctors gave me hope. It wasn't internal bleeding so there was nothing to worry about. But inside me, I still felt a sense of dread.

How could such woe betide me and my two year old kid?

I could remember all that had happened vividly, to this day.

It seemed like it was just yesterday I had been holding my husband in my loving arms, and now he was gone. I hadn't been able to cope with that. I decided within me that it was best we moved away.

My husband's killer was still lurking at that town and I didn't want him coming anywhere near my baby. She was the only thing I had left of my husband and I was going to do anything, absolutely anything, to protect her.

With that, I steered the car to a curb and parked. It was just opposite my house and it seemed pretty convenient-incase I had an emergency and wanted to rush out to the hospital. It wouldn't be difficult trying to reverse the car before I would hit the road. I sighed heavily and made to carry my kid.

Chapter 4

Dedicated to

I unstrapped the seatbelt that was cinched around Lisie's small frame, she clung to me tightly and began to sob. I sang to her and tried to coo her.

I could not help but worry, feeling the stress lines form across my face.

What was going to befall us in this small town? And why was that strange someone stalking me?

If I myself was pretty shaken by the events of today, I couldn't bear to think of what effect it would have on a kid, who was just five years old.

She continued sobbing and I just kept on petting her hair and singing softly in her ears. That seemed to work some magic because after a while, she finally quietened down. Her sobs now turned to hiccups and I kissed her soft hair. Holding her up just the way I used to when she was little, I used my face to rub her stomach. She squealed in delight and kissed my left cheek.

"I love you, baby," I muttered in her ear.

She snuggled closer to me and told me the same.

"Now, let's get you showered and ready for dinner," I stated and dropped her on the ground. She smiled and trudged her chubby little legs along the stone path that led to the house. Dusk was starting to set and the golden rays of the sun cast an orange glow about. The flowers that were planted by the side of my house, fluttered slightly in the breeze. Their bodies swaying here and there.

I closed the back seat door and picked up the scattered books that were strewn all over the car. That done, I put them in Lisie's bag and zipped it. It had been a really long day for me; work and taking care of my little kid, was taking it's toll.

I just wish I had some form of support, knowing it would help immensely.

I sighed once again, and headed to open the door for Lisie to go in and have her bath. But probably knowing who she was, I knew it would take a lot of begging and plays to get her to it.

Lisie had always been a spitfire right from her earlier years. She always cheered me up whenever I felt sad and lonely—thinking about my husband but, she was my strength. She was the one who kept me going and I couldn't be more grateful to have her as my kid.

I noticed Lisie tapping her foot on the ground, probably itching to go inside. I often mused at how she could act so mature at times in certain situations even though she was just a little child. Searching my hand bag for the keys and finally finding it, I inserted it into the door lock and a 'click' sound was heard.

Lisie bobbed up and down in excitement and flung her school shoes on the gray coloured rug of the sitting room, as soon as she entered the house. She looked so happy.

Hell, I wish it was so for me.

She held her hands up in the air, whirling and dancing around to a tune that was probably playing in her head. I chuckled lightly at that, the events of the day were now forgotten.

Kids, I sighed. One minute they are shedding tears, the next, they are smiling sunily like nothing ever happened.

Dropping her school bag on the brown, striped couch, I closed the main door and looked round, trying to survey if everything was still in place. This was indeed an old habit of mine and it felt a bit refreshing to take every single detail into account. It had always helped me get through the years and I knew it always would.

The house seemed just the way I had left it when I had been rushing to drop Lisie off at school earlier this morning.

Toys were scattered all over the rug. There were unwashed dishes which were clustered on the dining table, the telephone was dangling from the receiver on the wall, bright-coloured socks were strewn about and the chairs were upturned.

But upon a closer look at the cream colored walls of the sitting room, there was a huge hole and I couldn't help but wonder how that came to be.

"It's time for your bath, Lisie," I ordered. "It's already getting late!"

I just had about enough of the play Lisie was engaging in and time was also running quickly. Sometimes, I felt I was being too lenient with my kid. Most at times, she proved difficult and disrespectful and she didn't fear the consequences. I hadn't been trained that way and I definitely didn't want her going down that road.

I watched Lisie run round the house some more with a pencil in her mouth and I could not help but be amused.

How would someone see homework as something fun to do?

That was always how my baby took her book work. She would play around the house while doing it and in no time, she would have it completed.

I shook that thought out of my head and braced myself for the task at hand.

"Bath now!" I ordered again. Lisie stopped running around suddenly and scrunched her face before heading slowly to her room. Finally!

I flipped the egg I had been frying sunny side up and removed the frying pan from the fire. The egg was already done, so I added it to the plate of spaghetti on the dining table using my frying spoon. It hadn't taken me long to arrange Lisie's school items in her wardrobe and do some minor cleaning before I began cooking. All the while, Lisie had been doing just homework. Imagine that!

"And scrub that body of yours clean," I shouted after her. "Don't want you smelling while we eat!"

I could hear her grunt and the rushing of water in the bathroom. I was about to dish out another plate of spaghetti when I heard the telephone ring. I frowned.

That was odd.

The house phone didn't ring except when it was a call from Lisie's teacher. I pondered on that as I sauntered to where the telephone was situated in the sitting room and answered the call.

"Hello," I was met with static. "Is anyone there?"

More static.

Now, what the hell is going on?

I sighed and dropped the call, hanging the telephone back on the wall.

I saw Lisie walk barefeet to the dining table, her hair all wet and droopy on her shoulders. Her blue eyes twinkled with mischief. And I couldn't help but ask, "Are you sure you scrubbed well?"

She bobbed her little head up and down and I made my way to the kitchen to get her a silver fork.

I served my food and placed it on the dining table, my mind wandering far away.

Could it be that the person that was stalking me was the one that called to creep me out?

If that was it, then their goal was definitely achieved as I was totally out of my sorts. I rubbed the back of my neck, the act I do when I was worried and dug into my food silently.

Almost immediately, Lisie spoke up, her mouth stuffed with food.

"Who was on the phone, mommy?" she asked, furrowing her brows. She had stopped eating and all her attention was on me. "Was it daddy?"

I paused and stared at her in wonder.

How could she go and say something like that?

I sighed and dropped my fork with a clang. No matter how many times I tried to convince my kid that her daddy had gone to heaven, she would intermittently keep on asking about him. But could I blame her?

She looked at me with her lovely blue eyes and gulped slightly. "Why aren't you saying anything?" she asked.

I suddenly found my voice and spoke up.

"I am sorry honey, but your dad has gone to heaven to meet his maker."

I emphasized on the word 'maker' although I knew I was probably being too hard on her in telling her the truth so bluntly but I also wanted to at least maintain a hundred percent honesty with her. She was my kid afterall.

I watched her nod her head slightly as if unsure of herself and continue eating her food. This had sure been a long day, I thought as I picked up my fork and attacked the remaining spaghetti and egg on my plate.

Chapter 5

I think I was getting this stalking thing way in my head because, I was starting to have nightmares. Most came as vivid images and flashes that remained etched in my mind. It was starting to scare me. Unfortunately, I didn't have anyone to tell this to, and I was sure that if someone were to hear this, they would be creeped out as well.

On one particular night, after I had put Lisie to bed, I retreated to my own room to have a good night's rest and not long after, my first nightmare started.

I saw the black cloaked figure that had been stalking me all this time, appear and reappear, trying to get close to me and my child. It worked at first, because I noticed Lisie was no longer with me, she was gone. Just like that, woosh, vanished into thin air. I screamed and kicked and shouted. This all took place in my bedroom.

But when I started calling out to Lisie to come back and never leave me, I appeared by the roadside. I looked around and noticed there was not a soul in sight and there was a thick forest directly in front of me. I dreaded what was about to come. Was this about to be my last day of survival? Was I about to die? Was I about to be used as an exemplary? I ran my hands down the side of my face and heaved a deep sigh.

A screeching sound deafened my ears and I looked up at the dark grey clouds just to see huge bat-like creatures en masse, heading in my direction. I began taking steps back. Okay, I wouldn't call it that because I was on my hands and knees trying to get away faster from them and by now, they had gotten close to me. I used my fingertips to block my eardrum so the high-pitched sound would at least be minimal but, it didn't work.

I didn't want to die. I just wanted a peaceful life with my kid. She was my only hope, my survival and my driving force. I had to be alive for her, I had to strive to live because of her. But at the same time, I felt weak. I bent my head down and willed for the creatures to take me. I was tired of screaming and crying. And I also realized maybe, I might have even lost my voice.

So, when I felt a pure sickening pain from the flesh of my leg being beaten, I didn't scream or cry. I just gritted my teeth and tried holding on. Perhaps, I might be able to survive this. I may be able to get my kid back, and then everything would be alright. I didn't cry when the creatures pranced on my head, I didn't cry when their teeth pierced into my flesh, I didn't cry when I was being beaten with their wings, I didn't cry from the screeching sound in my ears. I just felt numb.

Totally helpless and unable to move. I knew if I did, the kill would just be more painful and merciless. I could feel my blood seeping out from my legs and trickling to the ground. Pain vibrated in every part of my body and I felt my life slowly ebbing away. There was no way I had any strength or will power in me left for survival.

I was floating. Floating into the deep calm waters and I couldn't see anything. Everywhere was dark and still, but, I knew I had to have plunged into the water during the feast of the creatures on me. What was happening? Was I being rescued? Or was I being left to die from all the wounds on my flesh?

I felt myself going deeper into the still dark waters and I told myself this was it. This was what the creatures wanted. They didn't want a human's existence. They wanted to take over and control the world. They didn't want any other living creature to survive apart from them. It was right then, realization dawned on me.

I was about to finally allow the darkness to take me when I felt a blinding light shine on me. It pierced through my closed eyelids and I resisted the urge to open my eyes for a while. Then, all of a sudden, I felt myself being pulled up out of the darkness that seemed to engulf me. I let myself be saved because, I knew perhaps life had another purpose for me.

Chapter 6

Zeal's POV

Central Park always gave calm to my daunting heart. It made me have this contentedness and satisfaction of existence. It was a brief experience that I definitely needed to clear my head and regulate my thoughts.

It had been five long years, years filled with sorrow, longing, dread, loneliness, and emptiness. I was dead at some point, devoid of any feelings and left with a void that constantly craved to be filled. The sad memories I had of these long years were even more than the happy ones.

That is sad, isn't it?

But still, I managed to keep on, to will myself to live, and move at the pace I had set for myself. The only thing I knew that kept me going was coming to the park. Seeing kids playing and having fun to their heart's content; creating the memories that would last forever in their minds was fulfilling for me.

Today was no exception. It was the weekend and as was the norm, I took my kid out with me to the Central Park. She always bubbled with excitement these times and would often share some of her fun filled memories on the drive home. I was happy that at least, she was growing fond of the place.

I sighed and looked up at the pale blue sky. It was clear and the sun shone brightly down on the earth, almost scorching and was intermittently calmed by the cool, crisp breeze. It was summer and so, the heat was at it's peak.

I fanned my neck with the collar of my shirt and turned my attention to a very bright and cheerful Lisie who was playing with some of her school friends, toys in hand and a stick sweet in the other. They were being supervised by some of the kid's parents who would often involve in their games and make fun of them.

I was totally fine sitting some distance away on a sturdy wooden bench and watching the scene before me, taking into retrospect the events of the past and how I had been able to cope with it. At some point, I got so lost in my thoughts and didn't notice the time fly by.

Lisie's POV

There was something my class teacher, Glee, always said. 'Everyone has their own story'. I knew that from my school experiences. Most times when my mom and I would walk to the Central theme park, I would see lots of kids with both parents having the time of their lives.

Holding a balloon and being dragged by my mom as we walked along the streets, I would turn and stare at the beautiful scenery. Kids laughing, parents taking pictures of them, smiles flashing, camera rolling, excitement noticeable. Even when we were past the park and walking to where my mom had parked her car, I would still keep staring, refusing to let go of the joy I felt seeing kids like me having both parents to cater for them.

I often wondered why mine wasn't the same. Why would my dad go to heaven and leave me down here all alone with just mom? Didn't he care for me? Didn't he love me? Didn't he want me? A tear would slide down from the corner of my eyes occasionally and I would stifle the sobs that threatened to escape from my body. What went through my head as we were crossing the street sidewalk was, if I would ever get to see him again.

If I would ever get to feel his arms around me and comfort me, if I would ever be able to brag to the kids in my class that my dad was coming to pick me up, if I would ever get to be relieved of this despair that quaked my heart.

My friends always talked about their parents; the various things their dad would do for them and their moms, the way their dads would always be with them on family nights or take them to the theme park, the way their dads would garner them to family outings or the way their dad would also hover around them like an egg's nest. My mom did all those quite alright and I couldn't ever be more grateful.

But I just wanted something more. I know that was probably being so selfish of me but wouldn't the work-load be less on my mom at least if my dad had been around, she would have fared better, her social life would have improved and those creases that were always on my mom's forehead would disappear...

I wanted to be strong for my mom, to not have her worry about my whereabouts every minute, to have her relaxed whenever it was the holidays when bad things always happened to kids my age.

My mom finally noticed that I kept on looking back and she tugged my hand and hastened her footsteps, muttering what I couldn't quite decipher.

I knew I was being so emotional about my dad and that made me overlook so many things my mom did for me. I wanted to appreciate her more, to be able to show her the love I had for her, but all I kept on doing was asking if my dad would ever come back.

Maybe one day, he would or maybe he wouldn't but still, I was going to keep that thought stashed away in my mind.

Chapter 7

Zeal's POV

I heard a loud chime that seemed to reverberate throughout the white washed walls of Alpha Cafe.

Alpha Cafe was home to all the inhabitants of Nellyville. Most of them usually came by either as tourists or as people who were running away from their dark past.

It was a small town and not much was talked about but, it was obvious that it was well knitted as most of the people who stayed here always acted like one big happy family. Gossips were the centre of attraction and not a lot went by unnoticed.

At first, I did admit that I wanted somewhere quiet, a place that one hardly knew and where I would live an unobserved life.

I had thought that this was the right town for me to start over, to wash away all the sickening memories of the past and to move on with my life but was it all a faux? I mean, just within weeks of me moving here, I was already being stalked by someone I knew nothing about. That itself, was reason enough for me to run away and never look back on my decision.

I knew I was being careless in overlooking some strange events that had been happening and trying to will myself to believe it was eventually going to be okay and I would be able to live in safety with my kid without any upheaval.

The whole town was brewing with mystery. Whispers and snickers here and there was always the norm, alongside bland looks which was enough to creep the hell out of one. But I refused to let it bother me.

Maybe, there was an underlying tone somewhere, something I was probably missing, and might have been overlooked. At the same time, I tried keeping my ears open for any news that would doubt my sense of reasoning.

I was pulled out of my thoughts suddenly; when the beardy, old man at the counter, placed the black, paper, cup of coffee I had ordered previously in a brusque manner.

I rolled my eyes, looking at him critically, before searching my black hand bag for my purse. He was a big burly man who looked to be in his sixties with white beard that covered the side of his face, chapped lips that looked like it had been bitten the hell out of, big brown eyes and a crooked nose. He had on an extra large sized t-shirt with a cream knickers that seemed to hug his mid-section nicely, and his stomach was protruding from the shirt.

The expression that was written on his face when I had first stepped into the cafee was one of surmise, as if I had committed a crime and was a suspect. I didn't let that bother me though, but I still couldn't shake off the weird feeling that seemed to settle in the pit of my stomach.

Finally getting hold of my purse, I zipped it open and took out some dollar notes, slapping it on the counter and taking hold of the hot, steamy coffee. He gave me a slight smirk and peered closely before taking the change from the counter and slowly counting it.

The sun was starting to come up and the drowsiness of the town seemed to dissipate. I used the chance I had to look round the cafeteria and take note of what the few early birds were doing.

From my peripheral view, I could see an old man who was dressed in a dirty sweatshirt and white shorts, holding a teacup to his lips and his eyes fixated on a newspaper.

There was another elderly woman who sat at the far end of the cafee, her gray hair was pulled up tightly in a bun, her face was filled with wrinkles and her eyes were constantly darting around. They seemed to collide with mine and I gulped slightly. The woman gave me a devious smile and a scrawny look that suddenly made chills travel up my spine to the small of my back.

I gave her a light smile in return and turned to collect my change from the counter guy whose name I didn't particularly care to know.

"Here's a fifty," he said, bending over the work top to stare at me.

I nervously took it and fiddled with my purse, my coffee now placed on the counter. That done, I grabbed the paper cup, feeling the heat embrace my fingertips, and was about leaving when I felt cold, rough hands hold mine in place. I paused and turned to stare at the man.

"Don't go nosing around in other people's business," he said, giving me a look of speculation. His eyebrows were furrowed slightly, and he ran his tongue in a meticulous manner along those chapped lips of his. I tried swallowing and felt something sink deep in my throat, making me almost gasp for air.

"I just wanted to let you know that," he concluded, letting my hand go and rubbing his gruffly on his shirt. All I could do was nod and make my way hurriedly out of the cafeteria.

This was actually my first time of making a public appearance since the three weeks I had moved in. Not wanting the stares and attention, I decided it was best to keep to myself and not go nosing around just like the beardy man had advised.

I pushed open the sliding doors and breathed in the cool, crisp, morning air. It filled my lungs and did little in alleviating my worries. I tried to shrug the thoughts of the events that happened earlier, out of my mind, and made for my car.

What I saw as I turned down the street corner, stopped me dead in my tracks.

Chapter 8

Her face was ghastly pale and the coffee she had been holding, now slithered and splashed on the cold pavement. Her fists were clenched by her sides and it was all she could do not to let out a blood curling scream at the sight that was in front of her.

The stalker, all dressed in black, stood a few distance away from her car, he had on him a small, silver knife that was gripped tightly in his left hand, and it glinted sharply in the early morning rays of the sun.

His legs were at least a metre apart and his arms were widespread as if beckoning on her. He stared at her and never for once, broke his stance.

Her heart began to beat erratically, she could hear the loud thumping and the exertive effect of her reflexes. Her eyes darted to where her brown, chevy was parked, the rays of the sun causing it's thick coated paint to shine richly.

What to do now, she thought.

She had to get to her car and hightail it or go back to the cafe and call for help. But who was going to pay her heed?

Besides, it was another stone's throw away; that was if the stalker didn't slice her throat before then and feed it to the bird choppers. At the same time, she knew if she went back to that cafeteria, there was a hundred percent chance of not getting any help. With the way the people there were unconcerned and gave her weird looks, she was sure this was going to be the end for her.

But. Lisie. She had to get to her daughter first. She would pick her up from school albeit early and then, pack all their belongings and take off. That was the thought swirling in her mind when she placed her right leg, directly in front of her left.

At the time, there was no one in sight and the street, reflected the sour look of the town. Her hands started to get a bit clammy and she could feel a steady pounding to her head. She felt her breath constrict and, it was all she could do not to gasp for air.

The stalker vanished out of sight and she let out a heavy exhale and made the short dash to her car. Once she had gotten in, she took a minute to calm her racing heart. The soft, rich leather of the car seat and the scent of cotton spray, seemed to assail her for a fleeting moment and engulf her senses.

By now, she was perspiring furiously as she put on her seatbelt and inserted the car keys into the ignition. She was about to begin the drive when all of a sudden, someone's blood was splattered on her window. She screamed and frantically tried to get the seatbelt off her.

It was stuck. So. This. Was. It.

This was how she was going to die.

She let out a scream and continued trying to unbuckle it; intermittently looking at the road for any sign of life. Seeing that she remained immobile, she started pounding on the window and calling for help.

She kept on flicking it's button that was in a compartment by her side, but it refused to give way. She began to cry hysterically, she couldn't imagine that such a paranormal experience would be happening to her. One that was only seen in books.

Tears cascaded down her eyes in rivulets and she bent her head on the car wheel, hitting it over and over again. Her head was pounding and her ears were ringing, she just discovered that there was no way out and all she could do was hope.

Hope that someone would come looking for her. She jerked her head up as she felt knuckles rapping against the windows. Looking round the car, all she could see was the red sticky liquid that was plastered all over.

She was supposed to be used to it by now, after all she was a nurse. But not when it was applicable to her, and her survival. Her eyes darted here and there as she kept on screaming and crying for help.

Her voice was strained and coarse after minutes of pleading and she decided to give up. No one was going to come after her and offer their comfort. She didn't even have a cellphone that she would use to contact the town's security officer.

She. Was. Alone. And the realization of that, drove a nail into her thick skull. Out of the corner of her tear ridden, red rimmed eyes, she could see the burly old man from earlier crossing the street and skidding to a stop as he saw her through the windshield. He halted his steps and when she thought the old man was going to help her, he zipped down his knickers and brought out his pee pee right in front of her; splashing his wee all over the place.

For a minute, she just watched, perplexed. Her jaw slackened and disbelief clouded her unbelieving eyes.

What the hell was wrong with the people in this town?

She began using her hand to signal for help, shouting and calling out to him.

"Hey, over here," she said, her voice croaked and high pitched.

He finished peeing and zipped his shorts, gave her a 'fuck you' sign and continued on his way.

Was he being serious right now?

No, this was fucking hopeless.

She felt like she was suffocating in the stuffy car and she tried rolling down the windows again. This time, it worked and she sighed in relief. The cold air blasted through and enveloped her.

Some of the red sticky liquid that had been on the window, was encrusted on the mirror edge, where it left a dent. She turned the car keys in the ignition and felt a wave of relief wash through her as the engine sputtered and came to life.

She inhaled and exhaled heavily.

She was okay.

She switched the gears and began her long journey to the only car wash in the town. She was going to give her baby a thorough wash, and leave it sparkling anew.

As she breezed through the traffic, her brown hair was billowed in all directions by the cold, early morning air. She felt chilled and rolled the windows back up.

On getting to the car wash, she spotted a block lettering on the stark white walls of the small, shambled building. It's colours were bright red and stood out, even from a distance.

It read simply, "STAY AWAY."

Chapter 9

Zeal grabbed a tissue from the tissue box that Glee had given her and dabbed at her teary eyes. She was sitting on a swing, rocking back and forth in the school's playground. Glee was staring at her in suspicion, and trying to offer the little help she could by rubbing her back, and muttering some incoherent words that was aimed at calming her.

Her mind was in shambles. She didn't know what to think; still reeling from the shock of the paranormal experience, she felt at loss for words.

This was not what she had bargained for, on coming to this town some weeks ago.

This was not how she planned her future.

She thought back to what happened several years back, and burst into fresh tears. Why was misfortune always befalling her, she kept on asking herself.

From her husband's death down to the strange happenings of the town, she couldn't help but feel her luck had run out. White sticky liquid kept on dripping from her nose and, she would use tissue after tissue to wipe it away.

She looked up at Glee through her red rimmed eyes which she had gotten from all the crying, and tried to give a small smile. Her jaw cracked in response and she felt her facial muscles constricting. She was tired of being strong, of holding on, and trying to keep her acts together.

She felt helpless and all alone. If only her husband had not gone out that morning, if only he had listened to her pleas, if only he had not broken his promise to her, then, he wouldn't have been dead by now. They would have still been one happy family, living without a care in the world, and none of this would have happened.

The list of if only's could go on and on but, she was pulled suddenly from her thoughts when, Glee spoke up.

"Zeal," she called out softly, her voice barely above a whisper. "Can you tell me what happened?"

She merely shook her head, staring at the well worn earth, and bunched her knees together. She was too weak to speak, exhausted from all the crying and drained of every drop of energy in her blood. It was not fair the way death had taken away her husband without reasoning, or being compassionate about her having a kid.

It just wasn't fair.

She could hear Glee heaving a deep sigh, overly frustrated by her lack of response. She knew she had to speak up, but at the same time, she couldn't seem to mutter any coherent words from her mouth.

A light breeze blew, caressing her exposed legs and billowing her skirt about her. She gulped slightly, took a deep breath, and finally decided to speak up.

"There's something strange going on in this town," she managed to croak out.

Glee paused for a fleeting moment, and a knowing look flitted across her features, but it was gone as fast as it came.

She cleared her throat, "what do you mean by that?"

Zeal clasped her hands and looked critically at her. The golden freckles in her honey, brown eyes, shone brightly in the mild rays of the sun. Her brown hair was knotted in a hurried bun atop her head and her small lips, were coated with a bright red lipstick. She wore a pink, long-sleeved shirt and a black floor length skirt that was tucked in.

She chuckled lightly, thinking Glee's appearance very professional as required of Nellyville's teachers. But she wasn't going to be deceived by the looks. It could just be a facade and not reality, she thought.

She snorted, "do you mean you don't know what is going on?" She arched her pencilled brows, and rubbed her hands on her blue, pleated skirt, willing the conversation to be over.

Glee merely shrugged and folded her arms across her chest. Zeal watched her facial expressions closely, hoping something or anything would give her away. She waited for a moment, confirming her suspicions and cleared her throat. She suddenly felt strength flow through her veins and it was all she could do not to scream her lungs out.

"Okay," she started. "Here is the deal."

She spent ample time in relating all her experiences to Glee, from her dreams, to the strange calls, down to the recent paranormal events. Glee would nod her head intermittently, taking in the pieces of information, and appearing to brainstorm.

Zeal concluded, "so we are going to leave first thing tomorrow morning."

At that, Glee paused and gave her a bewildered expression. "What do you mean you are going to leave?" she asked a bit loudly.

She knew it right then. The teacher obviously had something up her sleeves, right from the minute she enquired about Bennie, and was brushed off. Her hunches were correct, something was definitely going on in Glee's head.

"We are going far away," she said sharply. "This town isn't safe as you can see."

The daggers Glee sent her way was enough to make her recoil. But she knew doing that, was going to make her a coward, and she wasn't one by any means.

Now, the plan was to survive the rest of the day, through the night and be safe for Lisie and hers' journey early tomorrow morning. She hoped that stuck to the teacher's brain.

As if on cue, they both stood, their nose barely inches away from each other, their eyes bearing hatred and sending a slight chill but Zeal didn't mind. It was her, and her daughter's safety, she cared about, and nothing else.

A bell gave a shrill cry in the distance, and Glee pulled back and straightened her stance. "It's time I head back in," she stated cooly. "Recess is already over."

Zeal was shocked; the teacher had spoken as if nothing went on between them some minutes ago, she slowly took back her position on the swing, and eyed her warily.

"I don't know why you are doing this," she muttered, suddenly afraid for Lisie's safety. But she knew, it was a school that had proper securities in place and therefore, there was no need to worry.

Before Glee turned, and walked away, she muttered something that Zeal caught on to, and her mouth went agape.

"You what . . .?"

Chapter 10

Lisie's POV

It hasn't always been this way.

We had once been a happy family.

But since my dad died, I didn't know what to make of it. I remember those cherished moments, the ones that made my heart swell and the joy that was evident.

When I had clocked one year, my parents celebrated my birthday in a grand style. They did all sorts of things for me, they baked me french coissants, cake, took me trick or treating, bought me lots and lots of icecream, took me to the cinema to see a movie and, we came back home exhausted. My dad had collapsed on the couch and my mum, well, she sang me my favourite Barbie song, read toy stories for me and, tucked me in bed, wrapping her warm, fuzzy hands around me.

I felt on top of the world. My parents showed me constant love, they never for once shouted at me if I did something wrong as I grew a bit older, infact, those had been the best two years of my life. My mom was very happy and always bubbled with excitement, my dad showered her with lots of gifts, and would often come home with a present or two for me.

Then, the period where my mom's laziness got the better of her, we would order pizza, and those days were to live for.

I never witnessed any of their arguments or fights at any point but, there was this one time, things got a bit . . . stale.

I was supposed to be in my bedroom having my afternoon nap, but I couldn't sleep. That was because of the constant bickering my parents were having and, I had slowly crept down the stairs and sat on the cold steps, watching them closely. They were oblivious of me being there and that was because, their backs were facing me and I had taken a good hiding spot.

My mum was poking dad in the chest and screaming so bad, I thought my ears would bleed. I tried to listen to what they were saying but, I could only catch bits and pieces.

"Why did you come home late last night?" she asked, her arms folded across her chest.

Dad ran a discomfited hand through his sand, blonde hair, and sighed.

"What does it matter," he started, gesticulating with this hands. "I have always been there for you and Lisie. So, why does this one night have to get between us?" I could hear the slight agitation in his voice, his tone bothering on the edge of frustration.

"I am just scared honey." My mama's voice was croaked and I knew, she was crying. Her shoulders heaved, and my dad pulled her into a hug, and was kissing her hair, and muttering something in her ears. My heart broke for my mom.

I couldn't tell why she was crying. I never heard the reason for their quarrel, and after a minute of watching them in that same posture, I had crept back up the steps, and retreated to my bedroom.

It was a hot sunny afternoon, and I was perspiring furiously in the pink, chiffon gown my mom had gotten for me, for the summer. My dad's arms were linked with mine, as was my mom. We were taking a stroll through the busy streets, and I was enjoying watching the flapping of birds in the sky, the ringing of laughter and soft music, the tantalizing taste of my vanilla ice cream, and the different field games like soccer, basketball, volley, that were being played.

I squinted my eyes because of the harsh rays of the sun, as I looked up at my dad and smiled at him. He seemed oblivious and kept on pointing various places of exciting interests to me, and my mum. I wasn't actually focusing on what he was saying, as I just let my mind drift to the kids that were playing tags, out in the open field.

They all looked so happy, each wearing huge grins on their faces and goofy dispositions towards each other. That itself, made me smile.

I was pulled out of my thoughts when my dad hefted me up in his thick, muscular arms and kissed me on the lips.

"Ewww, daddy," I said, scrunching up my face in frustration. "You know I hate it when you do that."

My mum's laughter rang out and she pulled at my cheeks, making my face look crumpled.

"You're such a cutie baby," she said, making a face.

I always saw my dad as my hero. With his sand, blonde hair that was always ruffled, to his slightly crooked nose, down to his big lips, and macho stature, I didn't doubt for a second that he was the right match for my mum.

"And I love you honey," my dad said, giving me a genuine smile that stretched across his face, and reflected deeply in his eyes. A knowing look passed between my mum and dad, and I pressed my face into my father's broad shoulders, wishing this happy moment would never end.

Chapter 11

Zeal's POV

"What did you just say?" I ask, my voice trembling slightly. I couldn't believe it. In actuality, I didn't want to.

"You heard me right," Glee said, rubbing her hands gruffly on her shirt, as if preparing for a fight.

I felt a tear slip from the corner of my eye, and in minutes, the upper part of my white collar shirt was soaked. I blinked hardly, trying to hold the flood back, but couldn't. Letting it fall freely and blur my vision.

I fell from the swing to the ground, the sadness clawing my heart and my chest constricted, making it hard for me to breathe. I held my hands to my mouth to keep from screaming and shook my head time and time again, telling myself it wasn't real.

None of this was real.

I bowed my head in shame and let the sob rack my body for what seemed like an eternity.

I could feel Glee's watchful eyes on me, but I made no attempt to lift my head. My heart was heavy and bore a weight that I knew, would never be lifted. I began to understand that this was a burden I would carry with me, all my life.

"Tell me it isn't true," I mumbled, trying to string my incoherent words together so it would make sense.

Glee seemed to have heard me because, she cleared her throat and spoke up.

I looked up in turn for her to say, "yes, Zeal, I fucked Joseph."

My ears rang and hearing his name again, made the realization hit hard on me, and it was all I could do not to screech the whole school down. I gasped, my body shaking violently that I felt at any moment, my knees would give way and I would collapse on the sand, filled, earth.

Joseph was my husband. He had been for five good years before I had given birth to Lisie, and through all the struggles of childbirth, he had been there for me. I never for once thought that I would hear something as profound as this. It came as a shock to me, and I found myself going over all my past memories of him.

He had been so sweet and unsuspecting. Never for once, had I thought that my husband was cheating on me. There wasn't any proof; he had proved his loyalty time and time again, all through my period of barrenness. But there was this one time, things went a bit haywire.

I had been diagnosed of a faulty and poorly developed ovary, and although, I followed all the therapies and medications, it had taken me years before I finally conceived and gave birth to Lisie. The doctors were surprised and had told me, this was going to be the only child I would have.

Those years of hardship and pain was all I could think about. I forced myself not to remember the good because, I knew if I did, I would fall in love with those memories all over again and I wouldn't be able to see past my hurt.

I gritted my teeth, they gnashed each other and a soft whimper escaped my lips.

"Why didn't you tell me this before," I said, my voice now drained of all emotions and sounded hoarse even to my own ears.

She folded her arms across her chest and snorted, an evil gleam apparent in her brown eyes.

"What were you expecting?" She furrowed her brows and scoffed at me. I could feel the heat reaching me in waves, and I suddenly felt so enraged. I let the anger seep through my veins and cloud my thinking.

There was no need shedding tears over spilt milk, I thought to myself.

I lifted myself off the ground and wiped the remaining tears from my eyes with the back of my hand and sniffed, taking a deep inhale and exhale. It seemed to calm my nerves a bit and I could feel a steady pounding to my head. It made it ache so bad that for a minute, I forgot my retort and just stared foolishly.

"What else aren't you telling me?" I asked through clenched teeth. "Tell me now." My voice was demanding and rough at the same time.

I felt bile rise to my throat and fought the urge to gag right there on the floor.

She shook her head slightly. "Where should I start?" she asked lowly, her voice confident and a scowl etched on her angular features. Ooh, what I would do to wipe that devilish grin off her face, I thought.

I sighed deeply, trying to rein my emotions in so that it wouldn't cloud my judgement.

After a while, I said sharply, "start from the very beginning."

Third person POV

Zeal felt an excruciating pain that caused her to grip the steering wheel of her car tightly, and blur her vision with tiny dots.

She couldn't wrap her head around what Glee had told her a while ago. There was no way to think when there had been only bitter-sweet memories. Memories that were ingrained in her mind, the ones she knew would stick throughout time and be forever etched in her mind.

Tears fell freely from the corners and ran down her mascara. Never in a thousand years would she have imagined that something this sinister would happen to her. It seemed far fetched but then, this was the reality.

The reality that her husband had cheated on her with an ugly school teacher. One that she was sure was a mistake of creation, a disgrace to womanhood and a creature that was fit for the dark pits of hell.

She laughed sarcastically. After seven years of marriage, this was all she had to show for it. It was unbelievable, the incredulity stunned her and reeled her senses. She felt her head pounding and a nerve continued to throb in her mendula oblongata.

Where was she going to start from?

Her heart was torn in shreds. It left her feeling battered and her loving memories of him began to crumble from the auditory modality of those three mind boggling and earth shattering words.

But she was grateful. For those words pushed her from her dreams and heart felt moments, into reality, thus firming her resolve. She swore never to let any man into her heart again.

Chapter 12

Zeal's POV

Lisie was throwing one of her tantrums again. I peered at her through my reading glasses that was perched atop my nose, as the sunlight streamed in through the shutters of the window. It illuminated the house and gave it a refreshing feel, creating a lovely aura that seemed to lift my dampened spirits.

She was sifting through the clothes that were strewn on the green couch in the living room. I uncrossed my leg from the comfy sofa I was sitting and put the nursing book I had been reading on Peculiar Pregnancies aside.

I sighed, trying to relieve myself of the stress that seemed overwhelming and took off my glasses, carefully placing them atop the small, sturdy, center table.

I slid from the sofa and folded my arms across my chest staring at my kid in awe. She was a wonder and even the little things she did, went a long way in warming my heart.

Lisie bore a frown on her chubby face and wrinkled her nose, she sighed in frustration and turned to look at me.

"I can't find it," she stated, her eyes watery and her breath coming in spurts.

I walked up to her and lifted her in my arms, watching her face pucker in exasperation. I kissed her cheek softly and she wiggled her eyebrows in delight.

I smiled. Whenever Lisie was happy, I was too. But whenever she was sad, she often threw a fit that tended to bring the whole world tumbling down.

"What were you looking for?" I asked, dropping her on the ground and smacking her ass that was non-existent in her tight blue jeans. She faked pain as she held her butt and jumped on the clothes, sending some flying in all directions.

She folded her arms and started wailing, flailing her arms in the air and kicking her chubby legs.

"Lisie," I started, feeling the stress lines form across my forehead and I fanned my neck with my hand. "Can you tell me what the hell you are looking for?"

At that, she furrowed her brows and puckered her lips. "I can't find my pink cotton gown you got for me on my birthday last year."

I blew out a breath, my hair sliding down from my bun and gracing my slender, squared shoulders.

"Is that what all this fuss is for?" I asked, throwing my arms in the air to show the incredulity.

She nodded her head slightly and slid down from the couch, gently picking up the clothes that she had sent flying. She could tell I was pissed; whenever she noticed a small change in my tone, she would sober up and give me a sincere smile. That would warm my heart and all my annoyance would vanish in an instant.

After she had finished putting the clothes in order, I held her by the hand and we headed in the direction of her room. The walls were adorned with various cartoon characters ranging from Rick down to Sponge Bob. The golden rays of the sunlight trickled through the open blinds and cast a warm glow about.

There was a huge floor to ceiling wardrobe that stood at the far corner of the room and a chestnut drawer by the side, with an oval mirror that was perched on it. The colour matched perfectly with the drawer and the walls of the room which was painted a pink hue.

It was spacious and airy and the only thing that seemed to occupy it largely, was the king sized bed that was adorned with floral patterns on the wooden frame, the red feathered quilt, and the pink fluffy pillows that were centered.

I couldn't say I was rich but, I always tried to make my house a home for Lisie and I. I wanted her utmost comfort in every possible way and always strived to give her the best things of life. It had taken a lot of effort but I knew eventually, it would pay off.

Lisie plopped on the bed and folded her arms around her small frame, her eyes darting here and there.

I sighed dramatically and asked, "have you checked in your wardrobe?"

I felt slightly irritated that everytime she looked for something and couldn't find it, the whole house would end up in chaos. And it was not only that, but when she played as well.

She bobbed her head and I made my way to the wardrobe, sliding it open thereby disconnecting it from it's hinges. I spotted different varieties of clothes, ranging from her school uniforms to summer and winter wears, down to her tailored outfits, all ranged accordingly.

My eyes roved over a number of items before I finally pulled out of a hanger, the pink cotton gown that she had been looking for earlier. I blew a breath, and turned to stare hardly at her. She was fiddling with the ends of the bedsheet and frowning her face in concentration. Not that she had anything important that made her facial expression that way.

I mean, it was only a dress. I tapped her softly and she bolted upright, turning to stare at me. I restrained myself from smacking her ass as I asked, "did you actually look for the dress?

As her eyes landed on it, she squealed in excitement and pulled me into a tight, body shaming hug.

"Thank you for finding it, mummy." Her breath was barely above my ear and it tickled my skin and made me pull back almost immediately. She took the dress from my hand and in a flash, she bounded down the steep stairs, to the living room.

I sighed yet again and plopped myself on the bed. I felt a bit relieved as I tried to engage myself in positive thoughts and activities in order to forget about my sorrows. My gaze flickered to the windows where a soft breeze grazed my skin and caused a slight shiver to run through my body.

My attention drawn, I drifted to the open blinds on the window and stared below. The house was elevated in such a way that you had to look steeply before you would be able to spot anything.

I heard Lisie singing shrilly in the living room, as I saw a shadow sift through the woods in the far distance. I rubbed my neck, an act I always performed when I was mulling over something and shifted closer to the window.

I could see the wild flowers fluttering slightly in the breeze and I gushed at the sight of pink daffodils curled up on a tree branch. I sighed heavily and stepped away, thinking of a way to pack my belongings.

There was no way around that, I thought to myself, as I headed for the stairs and heard a blood curling scream.

Chapter 13

Zeal's POV

Flashback.

I gritted my teeth in pain as I held my baby bump and tried to make my way across the cold, well worn steps. I stopped and took a deep breath. Blood pooled from my legs and trickled to the linoleum floor. I gasped when I saw it and I knew this was a sign that the baby was going to come prematurely.

I gripped the golden banister and laid against it for support. I could scream but no one would hear me and that was because, I didn't have neighbours for miles away. The telephone was downstairs and here I was, struggling to get to the steps. Didn't think I would make it in time to the hospital.

But, I had to try. I heaved a sigh and began moving forward, my movements were disgruntled. When I finally reached the stairs, I painstakingly made my descent, barely holding back a scream. I was on the third steps when my right feet connected with a sharp nail that thrust through and appeared at the other side. I didn't know when I let out a blood curling scream and gasped in horror.

Blood began to pump out of the wound. Tears pooled from the corner of my eyes and slid down in rivulets down my face. I contorted my face in anguish as I screamed yet again, "someone please help me."

My voice bounced off the paster white walls of my home and ricocheted for miles. I sat on the steps akwardly and held my head in my hands. It ached so bad that it made me want a brain freeze. My gaze was drawn to the pool of blood that lay underneath me and lacquered the hard wood steps. It wasted no time in dripping down and colouring the white carpet at the base.

I saw my life flash before my very eyes as I slowly began to lift my leg from where it had been punctured. Feeling a sharp pain jolt through me, I lost my balance and fell, tumbling down the steps hardly.

Then, everything went black.

At night, Zeal couldn't sleep. She kept on tossing, turning and bunching the bedsheet in her arms, while Lisie slept at the edge of the bed. She had been positioned earlier in the crook of Zeal's arms but because of her bedplay, Lisie had scooted to the far corner and slept soundly.

Feeling utterly frustrated with herself, she had crept down the stairs stealthily and headed to the refrigerator in the kitchen to get a cold bottle of water.Flipping the cap, she leaned on the fridge, using her body as a wedge. The kitchen was dimly lit with only a sliver of light passing through the shutters.

Her legs carried her to the sitting room and she dropped the water she had been drinking carefully on the center table, and plopped on the comfy couch. Zeal thought back to what had caused Lisie's scream.

There at the exact same spot the stalker stood watching her, she had seen a little, blonde haired girl who had on a pink, sleeveless, flowered gown with a black hoodie that graced her head.

She held a silver knife that glinted sharply in the diminishing sunlight, using it to slice her throat, licking the blood off it, and slumping on the ash, granite road. Zeal hadn't realized who it was but she had to protect her daughter in any case that the sight would cause her harm.

It was only after she had settled in for the night that she thought carefully about it and concluded that the girl looked exactly like Bennie. Zeal knew that Lisie would have guessed it was her even from a far distance. That was because, they had been bonded in a strange way and till now, she couldn't fully understand it.

She could only hope that Lisie was the least bit affected. Zeal's throat felt parched even after gulping almost a whole bottle water, and she got a hold of it and downed the rest.She felt rejuvenated and laid down on the couch in an upright position and simply stared at the stark, white ceiling of a place she had once called home.

By the morning, they would be far gone from the town, never to come back. The suitcases that Zeal was taking with her for the journey, were already loaded in her car trunk and waiting for it to be dispersed. She couldn't wait to hightail it because, she was scared that at any minute, something terrible would happen to hinder them from leaving.

It was possible that Glee had cleverly planted a trap and she had to use her senses to her utmost ability. Zeal wasn't going to ignore her gut feeling just like she did with Bennie who was now dead. The journey was going to be a risky one which she knew quite well but it all laid on her.

The responsibility weighed on her shoulders and she felt it press deeply on her sub-conscious. There was no backing out, otherwise, they would be trapped in the town forever and she wasn't going to give room for the devil which was Glee, to finish the handiwork she had already started.

But, there was one problem. Lisie didn't have an idea that they were traveling far away, to a place she didn't even know. Zeal knew if she told her, that she would freak out and would create a tantrum. Right from the start, Lisie never liked the idea of moving to a new place. It irked her and made her irritated.

Zeal remembered the first time they had moved. Between then and now, a good number of years had passed.

So, everything was planned in the secret. While Lisie was playing ball at the backyard, Zeal had discreetly packed the suitcases and stashed them away in the trunk of her brown Chevy. She would lie to Lisie that they were going on a short tour and would be back before school day.

If there was one thing Lisie had a weakness for, it was vanilla ice cream and short tours. She absolutely loved them and would disturb Zeal ever so often, to take her to one. But she never had the time for such frivolities. Yes, Zeal knew Lisie was a kid and once in a while, that was inevitable but it wasn't to be done regularly.

Lisie had no choice but to respect her decision, since she was playing both the role of a mother, and a father.

Thoughts of what lay ahead kept on churning in Zeal's mind as she fell into a peaceful, dreamless sleep.

Chapter 14

Flashback.

"There is something you didn't know about, Joseph," Glee started, fiddling with the hem of her black, floor length skirt and eyeing me warily.

I released a shaky breath and looked steely into her honey, brown eyes that reflected composure and serenity. I had just about enough reveals in only a few hours. I didn't want to acknowledge any more-infact, it scared the hell out of me but, at the same time, curiosity was eating at my insides and pushing me to cave in.

I tried resisting for a while, biting my lips so I wouldn't ask any questions; questions whose answers would crumble me and leave me in shambles. But still, I had to know.

I swallowed visibly and bobbed my head in acceptance.

I was finally ready.

"Tell me," I demanded, bracing myself for the worst. Glee gave me a devilish grin, one that stretched wide across her face and the corners of her lips quirked upwards, as if in scorn. She was mocking me because, to her, I was weak and didn't have enough guts as she did.

Although, there was one thing she seemed to forget. I was a mother and I had duties and responsibilities, whereas, she didn't. Glee waited for a minute before she spoke up, "Joseph didn't die like you thought."

My eyebrow was arched in surprise, the movement caused my head to ache slightly and a vein continued to throb in my temple as I began to ruminate over the possibilities.

If my husband didn't die, then where had he been all these years I was struggling to fend for myself and Lisie?

My head was exploding with so much information, and I wasn't entirely sure Glee was telling me the truth about anything. But at the same time, there was no one to believe.

It was either her or nothing, and besides, she seemed to know more about my husband than I did. Despite the good number of years we had spent together.

"Are you trying to tell me that all I thought about my husband was wrong?" I asked, furrowing my brows and shaking my head in doubt. I couldn't believe it, the incredulity stunned me and left me a nervous wreck. I kept on biting my nails in panic and waited for Glee to give me an answer, as I continued tapping my feet impatiently on the ground.

After what seemed like an eternity, she heaved a deep sigh and said, "I don't know about that."

It was almost sunrise when we began the journey. I wanted to get an early start in case of any technical issues I would encounter on the road. The morning rays of the sun made the town hazy as I zipped past with my car.

The wind nipped at my lengthy, brown hair, flying it in all directions, while some stuck to my face. The cold, morning air bit at my cheeks, it gave me a slight chill and made me feel a bit refreshed. I continued to observe Lisie intermittently through the rear-view mirror that was between my seat and the passenger's seat.

She was oddly quiet as she sipped her orange juice that was in a small bottle, and pressed her face closer to the window. I began wondering what was wrong with her.

Could it be the odd incident that had happened earlier, I thought to myself as I approached a speed breaker and had to step firmly on the brakes. Lisie's head bobbed forward and hit the wedge of my seat.

"Ouch." I heard her yell. She used her hand to massage the sore spot on her head and scrunched her face in anger.

I muttered a "sorry" as the car progressed at a much slower pace. Out of the corner of my eye, I saw the can juice that Lisie had been drinking, splattered on the passenger's seat, the liquid was dripping slowly to the ground.

I heaved a sigh and flexed my stiff fingers on the steering wheel. I was beginning to think I was getting too paranoid about the whole incident but, at the same time, I had to be extra cautious.

Lisie lurched forward all of a sudden and began wisphering sweet nothingness in my right ear. It tickled me and I squealed in delight as the car swerved a little to the side. If there was one thing I hated;

it was being vellicated but, any time Lisie wanted to get me overtly annoyed, that was the means she seemed to devise.

"Stop that," I yelled, willing her to stay put in her seat. "Put on your seat belt now."

The way I snapped made her compliant. She leaned back into her seat, and folded her arms over her small frame looking out at the tall trees and wild flowers that was one of the physical characteristics of Nellyville.

"I told you to put on your seat belt right?" I demanded, blowing out a breath in exasperation.

She grumbled but slowly slid the seat belt over her body and remained still. For a full minute, silence reined and seemed to engulf the car. When I couldn't take it any longer, I stretched my right hand to put on the radio, and after a few clicks, loud music blasted through. I toned down the volume a bit and focused my attention back on the road.

My favourite song Senorita by Camilla Cabello was on and I was swaying my body, my head moving in sync with the rhythm.

Then out of the blues, I heard Lisie yell above the loud music. "W here are we going?" At that, I scratched my head with my left hand, keeping the right on the steering wheel.

Some minutes passed, before I spoke up. Through the rear-view mirror, I saw Lisie looking at me expectantly, curiosity brimming in her bright, blue eyes.

"We are going on a short trip, honey," I stated, my voice croaked at the edges.

"And where could that be?" she asked, inching forward from her seat.

I gripped the steering wheel in a firm manner and smiled briefly.

"You'll see . . . you'll see," I muttered, my voice inaudible. And with that, I leaned back in my seat and continued to enjoy the feel of the music.

Chapter 15

Lisie's POV

I looked up at the bright blue sky through the car window, silently watched the birds flying high in the sky. Their wings were flapping in the air as the chill, morning air blew my blonde hair away from my face and messed it, slapping them onto my eyes.

I took a deep breath of the scent of wild, hibiscus flowers that were arranged in a sequence as my mum's car drove past.

I stared at the tall trees that dotted the landscape as we approached the outskirts of the town.

Leaning back in my seat, I began hearing my stomach making weird noises. The upper part was paining me and I whined, my voice sounding annoying even to my own ears.

"Mummy, I am hungry." My voice was high pitched and I unbuckled my seatbelt and slid between her and the passenger's seat. I put my right hand on my jaw and simply stared ahead. I wasn't having fun anymore.

Mum didn't answer me. She just kept on driving and my stomach kept on biting me. I couldn't hold it anymore and cried out.

"I want food." I demanded, stomping my foot on the ground. It was then mum turned to look at me, her teeth baring white.

"Do you really want me to stop?" She asked, her eyebrows rising to the top of her head. "Because I am not going to."

Tears started coming from my eyes just then. "Why won't you stop?" I asked folding my arms across my chest in anger. "My stomach is paining me and I want food."

I could hear my mum saying something to herself, as she rolled up the windows by using her right hand to press a small button that was by her side.

She put on the AC and rested on the car seat. I felt a bit cold as the air hit me and made me hug my red, thick sweater closer to my body.

Mum wasn't going to answer me. I had to find a way to get her attention then, I thought, as I began shifting from one seat to the next and kicking my chubby legs.

"I want to pee." I whined, holding my private area and bending my head as if in pain.

I could hear my mum laughing. Erhhh, so she wasn't going to buy that?

I thought for a minute and then I suddenly had a bright idea.

"Hey, look." I yelled, pointing my right finger ahead. The car came to an abrupt halt and mum turned to stay at me. Her hand was still on the wheel and I could see the anger in her eyes. Out of the corner of my eyes, I noticed we were in the middle of the road with no one in sight.

"Seriously!" she stated, blowing her breath in my face. "If you don't behave now, I am going to throw you out of this car."

With that, I burst into fresh tears. I wanted to pee and I was hungry at the same time but, mummy didn't want me to do any.

Why was she being so mean to me?

"It's either you sit still," she started. "Or you stay out."

I didn't say anything. I just kept on crying and blowing my nose on my sweater. I guess Mum took that as a "yes" because, she slid the car into gear.

We were going at a much slower pace and I slumped into my seat feeling a bit bad. It was not my fault that I was acting this way. Mum refused to tell me where we were going and I hated surprises. They just made me want to throw up all over the place.

My thoughts went to Bennie as I resumed staring out the window. I was never going to see her again because, she was dead and would no longer get to play with me like she used to.

I missed her kisses on my lips, I missed the fun we had during school break, I missed the times we often did a game of hide and seek and I also missed our constant fights. Bennie always wanted to outsmart me in almost everything. She was good in reading, even though sometimes she would stay mute just to make fun of Miss Glee.

I could see her getting mad in my head and bringing out her fat cane to torture Bennie. I hated seeing her cry, it made me sad and feel a bit lonely because, at those times, she would refuse to talk to me.

Mum hated her. Or at least, I thought so. She was always driving me away from her and doing all she could to keep us apart. Anytime she came to pick me up from school, she would make sure I was nowhere near her and that became tiring for me.

I tried hiding away from Bennie whenever my mum was around school and she seemed to take note of it. I didn't think she thought much of it but, ooh well, it could just be me.

My mum turned on the car radio once again and my eyes flew open, knowing I wasn't going to get any sleep till we got to wherever we were going. She continued to click from one station to the next, static filled the car and made me block my ears.

I noticed my mum was not minding the road and paying attention to a stupid radio of which I had no use for.

"Please turn it off," I yelled. "Turn that thing off."

I was slowly getting angry. I caught my mum's eyes staring at me through the rear mirror as the car kicked up speed.

She seemed to sense that something was wrong with me because, she asked softly. "Are you okay, honey?"

My hand shot up to my ears in pain and my eyes grew wide when I saw the pool of blood that coloured my pale fingers.

"Arghh." I screamed as I saw the car swerve to the other direction and my mum trying to control the steering wheel.

There went a loud ringing in my ears as everything slowly went black.

Chapter 16

Zeal

"Mrs White?"

I struggled to blink back tears that threatened to slip from the corner of my eyes, as they slowly adjusted to the growing darkness.

I craned my neck to stare at the moonlight that shone it's light through the open curtains and partly illuminated the cold, dark room.

My eyes roved over the environment I was in. To my left was a gurney and a huge, metal table that stood by it with different tablets and sharp, pointed needles that almost stuck out, and looked too clustered for me to note anything perculiar.

That told me distinctly that I was in a hospital. I gulped as I turned my head painstakingly, to my right. There was a hospital bed by the far corner. It filled almost the entire length of the room and the spreads were well laid out as if someone just vacated from the space.

I slowly took in the garment I was clothed in. It was a starched gown of whose colour I couldn't decipher because of the insufficient lighting. The cloth felt stiff and didn't do justice to my slim curves.

It was fitted from my neck up to my small, firm breasts and then it flowed down to my knees.

I sat up with much effort, grunting at every ounce of pain I felt in all parts of my body. My head was pounding with a resounding headache that made me unaware of the golden chains that cuffed my wrists to the edge of the bed.

It was only when I tried moving my legs which felt like heavy pots of lead, did I realize that I was actually chained, the sound reverberating throughout the walls of the nearly- empty room. My mind was foggy, my vision was blurry and for a minute, I sat still staring at nothing and unable to form any coherent thoughts.

My head whoozed and I felt a bit faint. I closed my eyes for a brief moment, wanting to recall the memories of the past but, I couldn't. Nothing came to mind and I slid back into the thin, transparent sheets that covered my mid- region.

I only hoped someone would come for me. A person that truly cared about my existence and well-being at least. I felt a slight chill that spread throughout my entire body and made me curl my toes.

It was cold. Too cold. I rubbed my bare arms and breathed deeply, expelling a thin whif of smoke into the cold air. I was trying my best to stay calm and not freak out over the fact that I was chained to a hospital bed, my heart was beating rapidly and my hands started to get clammy as I kept on rubbing it over and over. My nails were scratching at the insides of my palm and drawing blood.

I could hear the crickets chirping right outside my window and I felt a shiver run through me and made my blood go cold. A fierce wind was blowing through the curtains and rattling the wheels of the bed as I struggled to break free of the chain.

I grunted in pain and kept on grinding them on the edge of the bed, thinking they would eventually give way but the chains remained adamant and as strong a hold as ever.

I knew if I eventually got out of this, the deep, cut marks that were engraved on my skin would last forever. I felt a mind blowing pain slice through my wrist as one of the jagged edges of the chain snapped and punctured my right hand. I winced in pain and gritted my teeth sharply, my vision blurred with tiny dots that seemed to cloud the room.

I didn't do anything wrong to deserve death did I? Why was I here? What did I do to warrant the paramedics bringing me to this cold, dark hospital? How do I get out? So many thoughts were running through my head at the same time; each one of them clamouring to overpower the other. I shook my my head slightly to get rid of any lingering thoughts as I settled in, trying to get some sleep.

Maybe when I wake up, I will be able to fully understand what's going on.

As I felt myself being pulled by the embers of sleep, I silently noted the hushed whispers coming from the closed door. It was too tiny and minute to decipher. I laid still, too afraid to move as I swallowed visibly and strained my ears.

I couldn't make anything out. The sound of footsteps was the only thing that was distinct as it echoed throughout the walls and slowly faded away. I was left here to die. To rot and go to hell, without a care in the world. There was no hope for survival. No way out.

I heaved a deep sigh as the reality came crashing down on me. A tear slid freely from the corner of my eyes and dropped onto my disfiguring gown.

I was too weak to move or say anything, infact, I felt my throat constrict and made me unable to form any sounds apart from the low guttural grunts that escaped from the back of my throat. My eyes grew round in fear as I spotted a shadow just by the corner of the door; staring at me. But, before I could think much of it, it had disappeared in a flash.

I was scared, I bit my lips until I could feel blood dripping from the tips and colouring the taste of my mouth, making me spit on the floor by the left side of the bed, and I shivered in fear.

I didn't know if I would ever make it out of this situation alive. I could only hope that 'hope' would be sufficient for me. At least for now, it was all I had and all I needed to keep me going.

With that thought, I let myself drift to a nightmare– filled sleep, bunching the thin, transparent sheet in my arms.

Chapter 17

Z eal's POV

"Mummy, can you hear me?"

"She is awake."

"Finally . . ."

I heard voices floating around me as I took a deep, sharp breath and my eyes slowly blinked open. The first thing I felt was the blinding rays of sunlight that flitted in through the open windows. The bedsheet was soft and silky beneath my pale fingers and a fluffy pillow graced my head.

I felt a bit at ease. The darkness was finally gone and with it was replaced a shiny light. I heaved a sigh of relief as I discovered that my hands were no longer bound with chains but, as I lifted them up to the rays of the sun, I noticed two red, jagged marks on both sides of my wrists. They glowered and discolored my white, transparent skin.

I noticed that my palms were a bit paler than usual, almost as though I lacked blood in my circulatory system. Flinching as I felt a cold finger come in contact with my warm skin, I gasped for breath in the blue, transparent mask that was fixated on my nose.

My eyes veered in the direction of the slim tube connected to the mask and glided across the white tiles with each wary movement I took. A green coloured cylinder sat by the far corner of the room and from my view, the tube was plugged into a golden valve that served as a passage way for oxygen.

I heard that tiny, incessant voice yet again, which was grating highly on my nerves.

"Mummy, can you hear me?" the tiny voice whispered in my right ear.

I grunted in reply and painstakingly turned my head to the direction of the voice. I almost sucked in a breath at the blonde haired girl that was peering closely at me. Her ink–black lashes shimmered in the light and her perfect shaped eyebrows were furrowed in concentration.

My eyes took in her appearance in slow motion. Her small, pink lips were puckered in exasperation and her bright, blue eyes were laced with worry. Her sharp, pointed nose blew gentle gusts of air on my skin with each breath she took. She was indeed beautiful.

In her red, velvet gown that contrasted with her pale white skin, she looked almost ethereal. My right hand flitted involuntarily to cup her left cheek as her eyes burned into mine. I couldn't recall who she was. I tried my best racking my brain but, all I ended up with was a sharp pain that resounded deep in my skull.

I silently traced my bony fingers across a pink, jagged scar that ran from the base of her skull to her forehead. The cut looked deep and glowed faintly in the sun rays. I swallowed visibly as I noted other smaller cuts that were spread across her pretty face.

There was one on her left cheek, another on her forehead and yet another on her chin. They looked fresh and almost distorted her beauty.

The little girl plopped on my bed. She looked tired, her vibrant eyes looked withdrawn and worry lines were etched on her forehead. I noticed a tear slide from the corner of her eyes. They dropped fitfully down her chubby cheeks.

She grabbed my right hand that remained stagnant by the side of her face and kissed it. They connected with her tears and I felt something shift deep inside me.

It can't be. It can't be that this girl is my kid. If so, why can't I recall? And why do I have this vague feeling in the pit of my stomach?

My thoughts were conflicted as I laid still watching her in the silence. Her shoulders shook and more tears cascaded down her beautiful face.

I shifted to accommodate her on the bed and pulled her into a bear hug, I kissed her strawberry scented hair and patted her back in between sobs. Her breath was coming in hitches and I could feel her tears dripping onto my hospital gown.

After what felt like hours as the silence stretched on and engulfed the room, I managed to croak out.

"What is your name? I asked, slowly lifting her small frame from her body and looking steely into her blue eyes.

She didn't reply me. Her eyes were now red rimmed and her lips had pinkish bruises on them. I guessed it was because she had bitten too much on them and now, they were screaming in despair.

She only shook her head and burst into fresh tears.

A loud creak of the rich, mahogany door startled us out of our embrace and we broke apart. I saw the little girl quickly wiping the tears from her eyes as she shot off the bed and stood ramrod straight by my side.

What the hell was going on?

I spotted a tall, thin woman making her way graciously towards me. I gulped as I instantly began to feel the bad vibes that were emitting off her and reaching me in waves. My hands gripped the edge of the bed and my gaze was concentrated on her face. Never for once wavering.

Her doe– brown eyes wore an evil glint and her heels clicked loudly on the floor and resounded throughout the room. From the corner of my eyes, I could see that the little girl's head was bent and her gaze fixed on the floor.

My heart went out for her. She must have suffered greatly at the hands of this wench standing in front of me. I saw her shuffling her feet and in seconds, she was breaking out of the room in a run. I flinched as my eyes connected with the frail gait of the woman standing in front of me.

One look and I knew she was evil. Her small lips which were coated in a bright, red lipstick were upturned and held a slight smirk, her nose seemed to be fuming in anger as they grew rounder with each inhale and exhale.

She had on a devilish grin on her withdrawn face and her gold ear rings glinted sharply in the rays of the sun. My eyes raked over her appearance.

But before I could note anything, she bent over me and her right hand which was coated with so many silver rings, connected with my jaw and my chin was rough- handedly brought to stare at her evil eyes. I felt a slight shiver run through my entire body and spread it's claws to my heart.

Her hand remained clenched on my jaw as she spat, "I have a preposition for you."

Chapter 18

Zeal's breathing stilled as she heard the loud clasp of thunder coming from outside. Rain was beating down heavily on the panes of the window as the car trudged along the street and meandered through the speed breakers on the road.

She couldn't see anything. Her hands and legs were tied with a thick, woven rope and her mouth was covered with a red piece of cloth that made her breath ragged every now and then.

The cackling sound of radio filled the car and she could hear the high pitched voice that sang along with the music that was being played. Zeal took note of a low guttural sound that was almost indistinct but, her sharp ears latched onto it.

This made her struggle against the rope that bound her hands as she tried to work them through and break free of the stronghold. After a while of pulling and scratching against a rusted iron, the only useful thing she could find in the car trunk, she gave up and closed her eyes briefly.

Willing her breath to come out even, she shot up from cold floor and sat upright. A metallic stench filled her nostril and she was just about to gag on the floor as the car hit a speed bump and her forehead connected with a sharp nail that was by the left corner of the passenger seat.

She let out a loud screech that deafened her ears and she blinked unbelievably. Her eyes were trained on the rusted nail that was stuck to her head as a tear slid from the corner of her eyes.

This was beyond an inhumane form of treatment. It was something vile and evil.

How could someone treat a fellow human being like an animal and tie them in a car trunk that was both stuffy and reeked of blood? That was the thought running through Zeal's head and more tears cascaded down her face. Her cries of anguish were drowned in the noisy background of the car.

Blood began to drip from the gash on her forehead as she slowly pulled it from the nail and a loud wimpher escaped her thin, pale lips. She gasped as she felt an intense pain split through her brain and her eyes slowly closed in defeat.

****

Hours later, the car had come to a halt and Zeal sat up painstakingly, she wiped tried to wipe away the remnants of sleep from her eye with her right hand which remained in a tight grip with her left.

Her whole body ached and her brain was foggy but then, she remembered something. Bringing out a small, switch blade that she had snuck from the metal table at the hospital, she waited patiently for what was to come.

A loud slam of the car door was heard and boots crunching on the gravel resounded through the silence that engulfed the car.

Crickets chirped in the distance and a low breathing caught her attention for a minute. It was that little girl. The one that was afraid of the evil wench, Zeal thought as she made a firm resolve in her mind to get her out.

The trunk door was slowly being opened at the sound of a loud key beep. Zeal held her breath and hid the blade behind her back. The blood on her forehead had caked and was a sore sight to see. Her hands started to get clammy as she began using the blade to cut the rope that bound her hands together.

For a full minute, Zeal continued to work through it until she heard a satisfying slit. Her hands were now free. She wiggled the rope remnants away from her and gripped the switch blade firmly.

The trunk door was fully open and the moon and the twinkling stars dotted and illuminated the night sky. Zeal felt a slight chilly breeze that made goosebumps appear on her arms as she rested her back against the passenger seat, her breath coming in spurts.

It was now or never. The evil wench appeared in her vision and blindly used her right hand to grope for her body. Zeal had squeezed herself into a tight ball to prevent her from being seen at first sight.

She could see the lady's claw nails roving in the darkness as she sullenly cursed under her breath.

Zeal held still and waited.

As her hand connected with Zeal's legs which remained bound, she dragged her out and was unaware of the weapon that she held.

Zeal's heart was thumping loudly in her chest as she slided across the length of the trunk. Finally getting close enough, her eyes veered away as she connected the switch blade with the skin of the wench.

A loud wail was heard and a body slumped on the floor. Zeal's nerve endings were frayed as she hurriedly cut through the rope on her legs and made her way to the ground.

She gasped as she saw the sight in front of her. The blade had connected with the lady's left eye and her right was in a daze. Blood gushed out from the wound as she cackled, obviously gasping for air. It took Zeal a full minute to recover.

A metallic stench suddenly hit her nostrils as she wrinkled her nose and turned to throw up on the grass twinkling with fresh dew.Firm hands gripped her right leg in place.

"Please do- do-n't ki-ll m . . . eeee." She saw the wench stutter as her eyes grew round in fear. The moonlight partly illuminated her as Zeal crouched to her level, staring at her in the face. She watched blood gush out from her mouth as a thought occurred to her.

This was the same woman that tortured Lisie, Zeal's daughter, and tried to pry her away from her.

Realization slowly dawned on her as her fists connected with the wench's face and her breathing stilled.

She was dead. And even so, there was still that evil glint in her left eye. The one that had been functional some minutes ago. Zeal felt a sharp pain slit through the hand she had used in finishing the kill.

But that not withstanding, a wry smile escaped her lips as she cried out in victory. Her voice echoing through the still night.

Just as she tried to pinpoint where Lisie was exactly, she heard a loud wail that pierced through her ears and stalled her in her tracks.

The mother and daughter reunion was indeed a wonderful sight to behold.

Chapter 19

The sun was peeking over the horizon as Zeal zoomed past with her car, her mind in a state of rest. This was the first time she was feeling at peace with herself after a very long time. Zeal had done something she couldn't have imagined having the power to.

She killed Glee. The woman who haunted her and resented her very existence. Her joy knew no bounds. As she whistled to a low tune, she smiled briefly at Lisie whose gaze was fixated on her. Her right hand linked lovingly with that of her kid as she continued the drive.

Feeling a sense of deja vu wash over her as her fingertips brushed that of Lisie's, her heart was almost overcame with a sense of grief. It crept up her sub-conscious and made her grip the steering wheel tighter as she struggled to breathe.

She tried but failed as a tear slid from the corner of her eyes and blurred her vision slightly. While she had been celebrating her reunion with her kid, she was oblivious to her physical impairment.

It was only when she called out to Lisie as she kissed the top of her forehead and brushed her lips against her chubby cheeks, that she realized Lisie had lost her hearing.

Her teeth clenched and baring white, she chanted her name but, her daughter continued to stare nonplussed. Lisie's gaze was concentrated on her, her lips unmoving and her eyebrows furrowed.

She had grown deaf.

That itself shattered her momentary feeling of relief. Zeal thought all obstacles that were hurdled at her had been relinquished. Little did she know, she had been wrong. The bleeding of Lisie's right ear before the car accident had spread to her left unknowing to her. This distorted her hearing and left her in a comatose state as she battled for survival.

There was no way Zeal would have known. She had been too busy trying to regain her memory and make sense of her situation that the thought never occurred to her. No signs were flashed her way. Infact, she had been totally clueless and left in the dark.

No wonder when Zeal called out to Lisie that day at the hospital, she hadn't replied but instead, shed tears. It was now realization was slowly dawning on her.

It was obvious that it was too late to do anything as they were headed on a journey to the unknown. Her plan was to drive and keep on, not stopping or looking back. For she knew that if she did, that would be the end for her.

Pain squished her heart and nestled deep within. There was no way to express her grief; the only manner she knew how was crying her heart out as more tears cascaded down her beautiful face.

Zeal didn't know when she released her hand from Lisie's and wiped her bitter-sweet tears with the back of it. She could feel her kid's eyes drilling holes into her head as she spoke softly, "Are you okay mummy?"

Upon hearing her sweet, angelic voice, Zeal turned and gave her a brief smile which didn't quite reach her eyes and protrayed the sadness that lay within.

"I am okay," she stated, affirming to herself rather than her as she kept on nodding her head unbelievably.

Disaster had reared it's ugly head and struck when she wasn't looking. It didn't matter that she had passed through a whole lot within the span of five years. To the outside world, that number seemed like a lifetime but not to Zeal. Those years had been a flurry of activities-all of which bore sad memories that dwarfed the happy ones.

Her jaw clenched as her inner mind played on the fact that Lisie could no longer hear her mother's voice. Zeal was going to have to learn how to make use of sign language, one of which she was a total klutz at. Back in the days, her mother tried to get her to understand it but, Zeal bluntly refused. There had been no use for it, she thought.

That was the end of their bickering before her mother passed away a year later. She being the wiser. Zeal heaved a deep sigh as she looked out the window in a bid to alleviate her sadness-not minding Lisie's quiet nature. The trees appeared as one they blended with each other and stretched for as far as the eyes could see. The grasses were evergreen and dotted the landscape thereby adding to it's effervescent beauty.

The sky was clear and the clouds billowed about the sun that shone brightly and sent a scorching heat to the earth. The hot air coming from the open windows blew her hair in all directions and some stuck to her face as her attention drifted back to the road.

Zeal made a resilient decision as the silence continued to stretch on. She was going to do anything to prevent further harm from coming to Lisie. This was because the little girl had passed through a lot and her childhood had been hell for her.

After Zeal's mum passed away, her father not being able to bear the grief and loneliness, absconded and never for once looked back on his decision.

He had been purely selfish. He didn't stop to think of the trauma it would cause to a fourteen-year-old. Moving from one foster parent to the next caused a deep void to fill her heart and frame her mudane life. Nothing seemed to matter to Zeal anymore. No one had cared about her existence-or at least, they didn't show it.

Zeal felt alone in the world and hid behind a thick wall that she had mounted close to her heart. The one thing every child dreamt to have was taken away. No love, care and affection was shown to her.

It was only after several years of hardship that she found a certain someone who tried to make life a bit rosy for her. When he stepped into her life, her whole world changed and all caution flew to the wind.

Despite her guarded nature, he had been persistent and before long, she had seen her resolve crumbling before her very eyes and couldn't help it. Joseph had stolen his way into her heart and helped her through all the dark times, he was always patient with her and was there every step of the way.

It was indeed a journey of self discovery for her. Zeal began to find some aspects of her life fulfilling and when Joseph bent down on one knee at the alter after a year of friendship, all she could mutter was a weak "yes" with tears in her eyes.

Zeal thought nothing would go wrong. His plans and hers seemed to intertwine and it was evident that the love they had for each other was beyond comprehension. Life was finally turning up for the better.

However, the one thing Zeal hadn't foreseen was where things would go a bit haywire.

Chapter 20

I felt a pang of guilt grip my heart and squeeze tight like a ball. Deep down within me, I knew it was my fault that Lisie had lost her hearing. A mother wasn't supposed to be so careless as to cause such calamity to befall her only kid but, what did I do?

The complete opposite. I allowed myself to get distracted and lose my focus on the road. Now, I was to blame. I let Lisie suffer because of me. I tried to relieve my mind from the shackles of being guilt-tripped but it wasn't working. I couldn't bear to look at my daughter properly.

Her bright, blue eyes was constantly laced with worry and looked deep within my soul whenever I spared her a glance. It was too much. I couldn't bear it anymore. I had to get out. I had to bite back the pain or I knew I would forever be trapped in an abyss. Endless circles of life and spiraling to the bottomless pit with no way of return.

Pushing back the incessant thoughts that troubled my mind, I tried to fix my attention on the situation at hand. The car had skidded to a stop in the middle of the road and no matter how hard I tried, it just wouldn't start. Surrounding us at both sides was a thick forest which bore an ominous sign and called out to embrace us with open arms. I didn't want to venture into that bush as my last resort.

Hell, there was no way I was getting in there with Lisie. I had enough to deal with as it was. I heaved a deep sigh and removed my seatbelt, watching it slide back to it's upright position. I removed the car keys from the ignition and was about to get out when a soft voice called out to me.

I could feel my hands shaking involuntarily as I slowly turned to stare at Lisie's inquisitive face. Looking at her brought back so many memories I didn't want to remember. I only wanted a clean slate but, with my kid always wanting to smother up to me-that was virtually impossible.

I gulped, feeling bile rise up to my throat. I couldn't hold it no more. I hurriedly got out of the car and threw up by the side of the ash-granite road. I took a deep, calming breath as I wiped my mouth with a white handkerchief that had been in my grip the entire time. Damn, I think I was being such a fussy baby.

I am a mother, I am a mother, I shouldn't act like this. I am supposed to take responsibility. My sub-conscious kept on reminding me as I put on a brave face and got back in, slamming the door in the process. I caressed Lisie's face with my right hand and pinched her cheeks lovingly before placing a soft kiss on her forehead.

'Mummy has to work the car to get started,' I whispered in her ear even though I knew it was a lost cause. There was no way she could hear me. That itself brought tears to my eyes and I hurriedly wiped them away so Lisie's couldn't see and start asking me questions.

I gave a brief smile as I clambered out of the car but not before motioning with my fingertips encircling my palm, for her to stay put. The only indication she gave of understanding me was her nodding her head meekly.

A gentle gust of wind kissed my cheeks as I breathed in the cool, crisp air. It filled my lungs and did little in alleviating my worries.

Raising the fender up, my eyes began to wander over the various compartments looking for what seemed out of place. I mentally went over the few details I had of car engines with a hand on my chin. Four cylinders which were the bane of existence of a motor in motion, was arranged in a V-line pattern.

The valves, spark plug, connecting rod, crankshaft, sump, and the piston were situated in their exact positions and none appeared to be heated. But, there was something else that caught my attention. A wire seemed out of place like it had been severed from a connection. The tail ends stuck out like a sore thumb and was a mixture of both dark red and black colour.

With my eyebrows furrowed in concentration, I peered closely and reached my hand out to touch it. A sizzling and electrifying sensation buzzed through me and I jolted back, my head hitting the roof of the car. I grunted in frustration as I held my now reddened palm.

"Fuck." was the only word I could mutter. The pain was excruciating and made me stoop to the ground. I spotted a shadow sift through the dark woods as I tried to regain my balance. There was no one in sight and the only sound I heard was the chirping of birds that sang merrily on the trees.

Looking up to the pale, blue sky, I saw hawks flying about, their wings flapping against the puffy clouds which portrayed nothingness. Something didn't seem right. I could feel it in my bones. As I scrambled to close the bonnet, a shrill cry pierced my ears.

Lisie was drifting asleep as her head slipped from the hand on her chin. It went back to the same position after some seconds, her eyes shut all the while. I heaved a sigh of relief as I went round to open the car door.

It's okay, it's okay, it's okay, I kept on telling myself, hoping it would calm my perturbed nerves. My hand clamped down on the handle and proceeded to pry it but, it didn't budge. I gave a deep breath and then tried once more.

It remained locked. My hands were shaking as I clasped the keys from my back pocket. I pressed a red button that was at the center and a loud beep was heard. This time, the door finally opened and I hurried in, shutting it firmly.

Lisie roused from her slumber and wiped her eyes groggily, her mouth was rounded in a yawn. I gave her a brief smile and motioned for to come into my open arms but then, her eyes grew wide in fear and she pointed at the window by my side, her fingers trembling.

She was quivering and shifting farther in her seat. My heart began palpitating out of my chest as I slowly turned to stare at what she was referring to.

The creature I saw made me give a loud gasp.

Chapter 21

Sweat mopped my brows and dripped down the side of my face as I gasped unbelievably. What the hell, I thought, my eyes growing round in awe and my stomach doing flip-flops.

Squishing noises were heard as I shifted away from the window, my body pressing closer to Lisie's in protection. The first whiplash of the creature's beak against the window was indeed a sight to see. I swallowed as I watched cracks slit through it, each varying in their length and proportion.

I was still. I couldn't move, my whole body was in a trance and my breathing came out ragged. Lisie squirmed in the seat, her hands shot to her ears as she gave out a piercing scream. I moved a bit from her and turned to stare directly into her blue irises, searching for what was causing her to panic and wail.

Oooh nooo!!

Tears were flowing from her eyes and her head was raised to the roof of the car as her pupils started to dilate. I bit my nails in panic, not knowing what to say or do. Lisie kicked her legs and began foaming from the mouth. All of a sudden, I sprang up from my position and brought her closer to my body, patting her hair and muttering a few indistinct words to calm her down.

I could feel her heartbeat pounding outrageously, her demeanor stiff and her fingers blocking her ear drum. She let out a loud screech as more tears cascaded down her face. The only sensible thing I could do was to wipe her mouth with a handkerchief and provide her the warmth my body offered.

After a while, she seemed to quieten and her sobs turned to hiccups as her breathing evened out. Her chest heaved and dropped with each inhale and exhale and I squeezed her tighter, eliciting a small gasp from her.

"Mummy, it's okay," her tiny voice muttered silently.

No, it was not okay. You could have died here and I would have been in misery, the memory forever etched in my mind.

I pulled her back and looked at her tear stained cheeks and red rimmed eyes. My heart clenched at how my baby's blonde hair was ruffled and a moist, sticky liquid dripped from her nose. I used my towel to wipe it off, kissing her cheeks one after the other and pulling her into another body- shaming hug.

I thought it was all over. Not knowing it had just begun. The creature prounced on the car fender, stretching to it's full height and my eycs bulged out of their socket. Lisie was clasped in my grasp, I didn't want to let go. My heart was thumping loudly and I knew it was no longer in it's right place.

The glinting rays of the sun reflected sharply on the webbed digits that were spread out. The head was contorted in such a way that the massive forehead extended in a narrow line to the back. There were no eyes, just a tiny pinch of flab that made up for a nose.

The creature's skin looked scaly and the colour blended with the evergreen forest. It's whole body was carried by a hunch which proved to be the skeleton that supported movement. The two hands formed wings which sprouted from it and had a flat edge.

I had never in my entire existence seen anything like this before. My breath hitched as it hollered loudly and Lisie screamed. I spotted blood trickling from her right ear down her finger tips and my eyes grew moist as tears began pouring out. I was scared, what was I to do? How was I to make the creature stop making Lisie bleed?

My hands were shaking as I frantically searched for something, anything, to block her eardrum. I heard a loud crack of the windshield but I paid the sound no heed. All I wanted was to get the hell out of here. Heaving a momentary sigh of relief, I latched the head phones I found in the glove compartment onto her ears and suddenly, she grew still.

Her head twisted to the side as she watched the creature closely as if attracted to it. It snarled and beat it's wings in the air, the feet moved an inch and connected with the windshield again and a thought occurred in my head. Why was the mere presence affecting my kid so much?

I mulled over that as I scrambled to get Lisie to safety in the back and just then, the glass shattered and pieces flew in every direction. I held Lisie in the comfort of my arms as my breath paused. My heart was hammering out of my constricted chest and my jaw was clenched in exasperation.

There had to be a way! This wasn't how I was going to die was it?

My stomach became queasy and I heard the driver's seat make cringing noises. That was it! It was in . . . I had to do something.

My eyes darted here and there as a low grunt escaped my dry lips. Immediately, the creature's head thrust through, it's head barely missing my leg an inch. It was crouched and even though the darkness was growing on us, I saw it's ears open as wide as the dam, the insides were in circles and steeped. My left hand shot up to cover Lisie's mouth so she wouldn't scream and drag her attention to us.

By some miracle, the headphone had fallen off Lisie's ear and now, she was groaning internally, her palms were clamped on my arm. We remained still as what I title The Beast strutted about and finally gave up. It retreated sullenly and I released the breath I didn't realize I had been holding.

We were safe. At least for now but we had to get out of the car or we would be done for.

The hair on my arms bristled and stood on end, I groped for the handle and opened the door. A cold, chilly wind hit me almost instantly and I stumbled out with Lisie by my side. As soon as my feet hit the ground, I hightailed it to the woods, my daughter hitched on my back.

I didn't care where we were headed. All caution had flown to the wind.

CPSIA information can be obtained
at www.ICGtesting.com
Printed in the USA
LVHW080516301222
736096LV00035B/922

9 781837 614721